The Magic Crystals

CHARMSEEKERS: BOOK SEVEN

The Magic Crystals

Amy Tree

Illustrated by Gwen Millward

Orion
Children's Books

First published in Great Britain in 2008
by Orion Children's Books
a division of the Orion Publishing Group Ltd
Orion House
5 Upper St Martin's Lane
London WC2H 9EA
An Hachette Livre Company

1 3 5 7 9 8 6 4 2

The Orion Publishing Group's policy is to use papers
that are natural, renewable and recyclable products and
made from wood grown in sustainable forests. The logging
and manufacturing processes are expected to conform to
the environmental regulations of the country of origin.

A catalogue record for this book is
available from the British Library.

ISBN: 978 1 84255 655 9

Printed and bound in the UK by
CPI Mackays, Chatham ME5 8TD

www.orionbooks.co.uk

For Imogen and Neil – with love

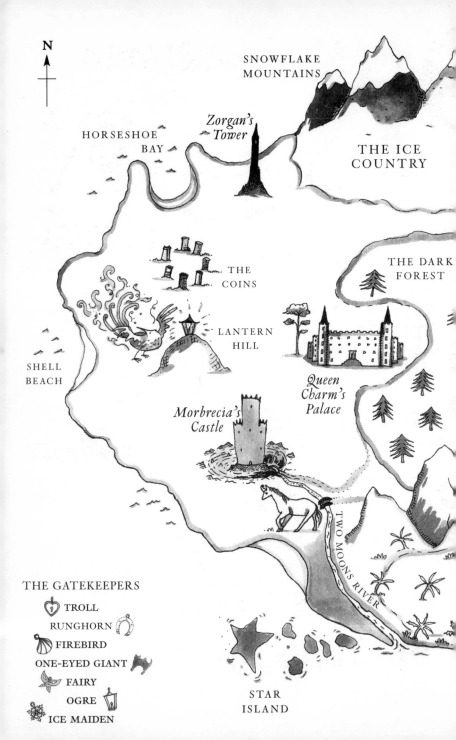

KARISMA

CAPE CAT

CLOVER FIELDS

HEARTMOOR

DOLPHIN BAY

MOUNT ORTUNA

The Silver Pool

KEY POINT

SWAMPS

JUNGLE

MERMAID ROCK

BUTTERFLY BAY

The Thirteen Charms of Karisma

When Charm became queen of Karisma, the wise and beautiful Silversmith made her a precious gift. It was a bracelet. On it were fastened thirteen silver amulets, which the Silversmith called 'charms', in honour of the new queen.

It was part of Karisma law. Whenever there was a new ruler the Silversmith made a special gift, to help them care for the world they had inherited. And this time it was a bracelet. She told Queen Charm it was magical because the charms held the power to control the forces of nature and keep everything in balance. She must take the greatest care of them. As long as she, and she alone, had possession of the charms all would be well.

And so it was, until the bracelet was stolen by a spider, and fell into the hands of Zorgan, the magician. Then there was chaos!

One

Sesame Brown woke one morning, threw off her duvet and jumped out of bed. When she looked out of the window, her big brown eyes opened wide with surprise. It was snowing! Thick, white snowflakes spiralled down and settled on trees, rooftops and hedges. They piled up and covered everything in a glistening eiderdown of dazzling brilliance.

"Yippee!" cried Sesame, grabbing her teddy, Alfie, and dancing round the room. "Snow, snow, snow!" she sang happily, at the top of her voice.

Her dad looked round the door.

"You're bonkers!" said Nic, and laughed. "Come down for breakfast, Ses. We're going to the park. I want to take some pictures—"

"Ooo! Can I try out my toboggan, Dad?" asked Sesame. "Can I ask Maddy to come? *Please*."

"Fine," said Nic. "We'll pick Maddy up on the way. Say about ten? But we can't stay too long. I must send some pix by lunchtime."

Nic Brown was a press photographer for THE DAILY TIMES, so Sesame was used to him always being in a rush to meet deadlines. Nic went downstairs to make coffee, leaving Sesame to get ready. She checked the time on her smart new watch (a Christmas present from her dad) then quickly texted Maddy:

Maddy replied almost immediately:

HI! CAN U CUM SLEDGING IN THE PARK? WE WILL PICK U UP AT 10. MWAH MWAH SES :)

KL! MUM SAYS YES. CNT W8. CU L8R LOL MADDY XX :) :)

4

After breakfast,
Sesame pulled on a pair of
fur-lined boots, zipped up the warm jacket
her gran had given her and wound a pink and pale
green stripy scarf round her neck. It was a present
from her riding teacher, Jodie Luck. Sesame thought
Jodie must have chosen the scarf with care, because
it was just her style! For a moment she stood
thinking about her dad and Jodie, who had been
seeing quite a lot of each other during the
Christmas holidays. They seemed very happy
together. She was pleased for her dad and had grown

to like Jodie, more and more . . . A shout from Nic at the foot of the stairs roused Sesame from her daydream:

"Hurry up, Ses! I'll wait for you in the car."

"Down in five!" she promised.

Hastily, she rummaged in a drawer for a pair of purple mittens and earmuffs, then looked in the mirror.

"Oh, no," she said. "I've forgotten my necklace." It was her favourite, a silver chain and locket, with pictures of her parents inside. It was in its usual place on her beside table, lying next to her special jewellery box.

The box where she had put (for safekeeping) the bracelet and six silver charms belonging to Queen Charm. Sesame was anxious about the seven charms still missing.

"I hope I go back to Karisma soon," she said aloud, as she put her necklace on. "I *must* find all the charms!" The clasp closed with a reassuring *click*, but Sesame checked it again to be sure it was securely fastened. I don't want to lose my locket in the snow, she thought, as she hurried downstairs to pick up her toboggan.

Outside it was unusually quiet and still. Sesame liked the sound of the snow crunching beneath her boots as she made her way to the car. *Crunch, crunch, crunch!* She smiled at Chips and Pins, who were gingerly stepping across the snow-covered lawn, leaving trails of tiny paw prints, and when some snowflakes settled on her eyelashes she brushed them away, laughing.

"Dad," she said, climbing into the back of the car and fastening her seatbelt. "Did you know that every snowflake is different? We did this project at school and Mrs Wilks told us that no two snowflakes are exactly alike."

"How does Mrs Wilks know?" said Nic, starting the engine. "Don't tell me she's checked them all!"

Sesame rolled her eyes.

"D-A-D! It's true."

Maddy Webb lived on the other side of town. Sesame often wished her best friend lived closer, because they did absolutely everything together. When Nic pulled up outside her house just before ten,

Maddy was already waiting for them on the doorstep. She kissed her mum goodbye, then trudged through snow to the car.

"You look gorge!" said Sesame, admiring Maddy's ice-blue top and hood, trimmed with fun-fur.

"Thanks," said Maddy, striking a pose like a fashion model. "Present from Mum. Oh, I love your scarf—"

"Come on," said Nic. "Or the snow will melt. Once you two start talking about clothes, you never stop!"

"Wheeeeeeee!" yelled Sesame and Maddy, whizzing down a slippery slope for the umpteenth time. They landed with a *bump* at Nic's feet.

"Time to go," he said, glancing at his watch. "I've got some great shots of people skating. The lake's completely frozen. I must send them to the picture editor—"

"Just *one* more go, Dad," implored Sesame.

"S-e-s—"

"*PLEASE!*"

"Okay," said Nic, half-distracted selecting pictures on his digital camera and resetting the lens

to zoom. "Once more. I'll take your picture as you come down."

Sesame hugged him and scrambled up the slope after Maddy. The girls positioned the toboggan so they could get a good clear run, with Sesame sitting in front and Maddy behind.

"Ready?" said Sesame.

Maddy wrapped her arms around Sesame's waist.

"Let's go!"

The toboggan slid over the glassy surface, faster than ever. The girls shrieked with the thrill of the speed, the wind whistling in their ears and snow-spray stinging their cheeks. Faster and faster they flew, until *crump!* They landed in a snowdrift, which had mysteriously appeared from nowhere. It exploded into a million crystals that sparkled like diamonds in the sun. To their surprise, the snow didn't feel wet or cold – it was more like falling into a cloud of cotton wool. Sesame felt her necklace tingle and next thing she knew, she and Maddy were whirling around in a flurry of snowflakes. Sesame gasped. She was sure, without the shadow of a doubt, they were on their way to Karisma.

"Maddy!" she heard herself cry as she tumbled head-over-heels through the snow.

"S-e-s-a-m-e!" came Maddy's tiny voice from far away.

The Charmseekers were off on another adventure, to search for the missing charms!

Two

Nix had failed in her mission to snatch Sesame's locket. The pixie had tried, but Sesame had got away in a magic balloon with three of her friends. When Nix returned to Zorgan empty-handed, the magician had been furious . . .

"Useless magwort!* I programmed you to carry out my orders, not to FAIL!"

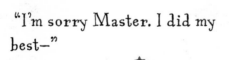

"I'm sorry Master. I did my best—"

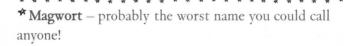

* **Magwort** – probably the worst name you could call anyone!

"Well, your best wasn't good enough, you idle doofer!* You shall be punished. Go to my library and dust ALL my books. There are five-thousand-six-hundred-and-ninety-nine. Ha! That should teach you a lesson. Get busy and don't stop till you've finished . . ."

And Nix had been dusting ever since.

Now, as Zorgan looked from his Star Room at the top of his tower, his attention turned back to Charm's bracelet. His head swam with visions of what he would do once he had control of the magical charms. Morbrecia would have to become queen and wear the bracelet, because the Silversmith had made very sure it wouldn't work for him!

* *
*Doofer – idiot of the first order. Brainless

13

Thoughtfully he rubbed the sore place on his wrist, where the charm bracelet had once burned him.

"Once Morbrecia has the bracelet, I'll empower it with Dark Magic. Then *I* shall be in control of its forces!"

Zorgan shook his head and stroked his pet bandrall,* Vanda.

* * * * * * * * * * * *
✶ **Bandrall** – rare flying
mammal, native to Karisma

"Enough daydreaming!" he muttered. "It's time to plan my next move. Hushish!* So much depends on my taking possession of Sesame Brown's special locket. I must hold it, to put her under my spell. Then the Silversmith will lose contact with her special Seeker and Sesame will bring *me* the charms! Hm! I *wish* I knew where she's hiding the ones she's found. I've no doubt she'll be back to look for the others. And when she is, I'll be waiting for her!"

* *
*Hushish – a word used to express dismay

Three

The icehouse was amazing. After falling through a silvery mist, the girls landed in a vast hall where the glassy floors and walls were made entirely of blue-green ice. In the middle was a dome, with thirteen numbers and words carved around its base.

"Wow!" said Sesame. "Where are we?"

"In a jolly cold place," said Maddy. "Oh, who's that?"

Sesame turned to see a young woman gliding towards them. She was wearing a dress spun from fine, frosty threads, which sparkled like tinsel on a Christmas tree. She looked beautiful, but Sesame thought she must be sad because what appeared to be tears were trickling down her lovely cheeks.

"I think she's crying!" she whispered to Maddy. To her embarrassment, her words echoed round the hall. *S-H-E -'S C-R-Y-I-N-G C-R-Y-I-N-G C-R-Y-I-N-G!*

"I'm not crying," said the woman. "I'm melting!"

"I'm sorry," said Sesame. "I didn't mean to be rude."

"Gosh," said Maddy. "How awful."

The girls introduced themselves, and the woman knew at once they were Charmseekers. "Fairday,* welcome to the Ice Country!" she said. "I'm Gatekeeper Seven. I'm known as the Ice Maiden. But if I go on melting . . . "

"But why *are* you melting?" asked Sesame.

"Things started to go wrong the day Queen Charm's bracelet was stolen," said the Ice Maiden, wiping a drop of water from her chin. "Since the thirteen silver charms were lost, the climate has changed and now I'm much too warm."

"It's weird," said Maddy, watching her breath make little clouds of vapour. "It feels cold as a freezer to me."

* * * * * * * * * * * * * * * *

✶ Fairday – a typical Karisman friendly greeting

17

"Yes, I expect it does," said the Ice Maiden. "But even a small rise in temperature makes a difference to us here. It's a slow business but it's happening all the same. Take my friend Karvig, the Snow Bear. He is suffering, poor thing, because the ice is melting and his habitat is being destroyed. He has to go further and further from his cave to hunt for food. Karvig *hates* warm weather!"

"I think something similar is happening in our world," said Sesame. "I read about Polar Bears in my *Wild About Wildlife* magazine. They're an endangered species!"

"I'm very sorry to hear it," said the Ice Maiden, as yet another tear trickled down her cheek. "On Karisma, the thirteen magical charms helped to control the forces of nature. *Together* they kept everything in balance. Since they've been lost, it's been chaos—" She broke off suddenly and shook her head. "Silly me! Why am I telling you this? You're Charmseekers! You must know all about the charms."

"We know the charms are special," said Sesame. "But we had no idea *why* it was so important for them to be together."

"We've found six!" said Maddy.

"They're safe in my jewellery box at home," explained Sesame. "Seven charms are still missing. We *must* find them!"

"Which ones are they?" asked the Ice Maiden.

Maddy remembered four:

"The coin, star, dolphin and cloverleaf—"

"Moon, key and . . . snowflake," said Sesame, pausing for a split-second before saying the last one. An interesting idea had dawned on her. "We're in the Ice Country, right? It's possible we might find the snowflake charm here."

"You may be right," said the Ice Maiden, with a smile. "Keep your ears and eyes open for clues."

"I will," said Sesame, excited at the prospect of finding another charm. "Sesame Brown will track it down! I can't wait to get started. What time do we have to be back?"

"By the Meeting of the Moons," said the gatekeeper.

"This is the mede* of Nerox, the seventh mede in our calendar. It's the time of year when the two moons of Karisma pass each other in a total eclipse. And today is the day!"

While the gatekeeper had been talking, Maddy had noticed the word 'Nerox' carved at the base of the dome.

* *
✶ Mede – month

19

It was one of the words they'd spotted earlier; she guessed the other twelve were medes too, because there was a verse written on the walls:

A TIME FOR WINTER, ICE AND SNOW,
A TIME FOR SPRING AND CROPS TO GROW.
A TIME FOR SUMMER'S RIPENING SUN –
A TIME FOR AUTUMN, BEFORE THE YEAR IS DONE

Meanwhile, Sesame could see a puddle of water forming at the Ice Maiden's feet. It was clear she was melting fast! Sesame *SO* wanted to help the gatekeeper, but how? Even if they found all the missing charms at once, she reasoned, it would probably be too late to save her. It seemed hopeless.

"Is there anything we can do to help you?" she asked.

The Ice Maiden sighed. There *was* something, but she knew it would mean placing the Charmseekers in great danger.

"Anything?" prompted Maddy, catching Sesame's worried expression.

"Well," said the Ice Maiden. "There are three crystals that are so cold they will stop me melting. I'm afraid their magic is not powerful enough to save the Ice Country. Only the precious charms can do that. But the crystals would help me."

"Where are they?" asked Sesame.

"In a grotto, deep inside a mountain," said the Ice Maiden. "But if you touch the wrong ones, you'll turn into pillars of ice!"

Four

The Silversmith paced the floor of her workshop, thinking. Thinking! She passed the thirteen magic candles; seven burn brightly for their missing charms, and her thoughts turned to her Seeker. She can't explain it, but her mystic powers tell her that Sesame is not so far away. And she's not alone. She and her friend are in a very cold place.

"Ah!" she said to herself, tossing back her long, silver hair. "I think Sesame may be in our beautiful Ice Country." Quicksilver thoughts darted like fireflies through her head, and she held in her mind the image of the magicial snowflake charm. It was a long time ago when she had made the perfect silver snowflake and the other twelve charms, here in her workshop. And now she sensed the lost snowflake charm was somewhere icy cold . . .

Suddenly her thoughts were shattered by the vision of Zorgan – bursting into her head like a bad dream.

"Tell me where Sesame has taken the charms. I know they're somewhere in the Outworld.* Supposing your special Seeker plans to keep them for herself? Then what? Tell me what I need to know, Silversmith. We could help each other . . ."

"No! Never! I know you're planning something, Zorgan. Your sinister schemes fill my mind like a nightmare. Balam** magician! If you dare harm Sesame. If you put her under a spell . . ."

"Curses on you, Silversmith. You'll regret you trusted Sesame Brown. You'll see!"

* Outworld – the name Karismans call our world
** Balam – cursed or damned

24

The terrifying image of Zorgan vanished, and the Silversmith breathed a sigh of relief. "Two can play at mind games, Zorgan," she said. "And this time I've proved the better player!"

But she knew Zorgan wouldn't give up.

Five

"Fantastic!" shouted Sesame.

"Totally brill!" yelled Maddy.

The Charmseekers were sitting side by side in a sleigh, going at a terrific speed across dazzling white snowfields. The sleigh belonged to the Ice Maiden, and was being drawn by a pretty dappled-grey pony called Frosty. She reminded Sesame of her favourite pony, Silver, at Jodie's riding stables.

"Frosty will take you as far as the crevasse," the Ice Maiden had told them. "From there you must continue on foot to the Snowflake Mountains."

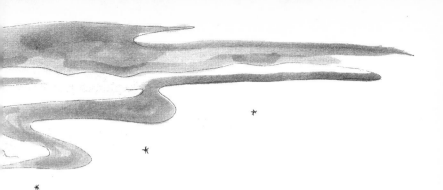

Maddy was clutching a small glass casket the gatekeeper had given her. "To put the crystals in," she had said.

For a while the girls sat back and enjoyed their dash through the winter wonderland of the Ice Country. They felt exhilarated, skimming along through plumes of snow, while over their heads an amazing display of trembling lights danced in the sky. It was a breathtaking sight.

"Wow!" exclaimed Sesame, as swathes of incandescent orange, pink and green folds swept the sky, like shimmering curtains of light.

"It's an aurora," said Maddy.

"I saw a TV programme once about the Northern Lights. They looked like this."

All too soon their sleigh ride came to an end. Frosty stopped by a narrow ice bridge, which crossed a crevasse, and the girls got out. They patted the pony and thanked her, before she turned for home.

Sesame went to the edge of the crevasse and peered over. She gasped in horror.

"It's VERY deep! I can't see the bottom."

"Ooo!" moaned Maddy. "I feel dizzy. Do we *have* to cross it?"

On the far side the girls could see the Snowflake Mountains, and on the near side the snowfields stretched away in the distance.

28

In between lay the chasm, with no other crossing place in sight.

"There's no other way," said Sesame. "We *have* to get to the mountains. The grotto is there somewhere. Follow me. You'll be okay."

It was terrifying.
The ice bridge was slippery.
The frozen layers were covered with a sugaring of crisp snow, and there was nothing to prevent the girls falling into the yawning ravine below. Slowly, Sesame put one foot in front of the other, testing the firmness of the ice with every step. *Crunch, crunch, crunch!* What if it breaks? she thought. No! *Don't* think. Just keep going! Maddy was close behind. Every now and then Sesame heard her whimper, and knew how frightened she must be.

"We're nearly there," she said. "Don't look down. You're doing brilliantly. Only a few more steps—"

"Aaaaaagh!"

Both girls shrieked in terror. Sesame had slipped and was lying flat on her back – one leg dangling over the drop. One wrong move, and I'm gone! she thought.

"D-d-don't m-m-m-move," said Maddy. "I'm c-c-c-coming."

She went down on her hands and knees and crawled towards Sesame, her fear of heights suddenly forgotten. Rescuing Sesame was all she could think about.

"Give me your hand," said Maddy. "I'll pull you away from the edge."

"I'm scared I'll fall," wailed Sesame. "I'm slipping—"

"Hand," said Maddy. "Now!"

Just in time, Sesame shot out her arm and Maddy grabbed her by the wrist; then she heaved with all her strength and pulled Sesame to safety.

"Phew!" said Sesame. "That was close. Thanks, Maddy. You were awesome!"

After the drama of crossing the crevasse the girls felt a bit shaky, but they hurried on to the Snowflake Mountains. Before long they reached the foothills and found themselves walking through a pine forest, where the branches were decked with snow. The air was very still. Once or twice they thought they felt a vibration along the forest floor – as if something very big was moving about.

"Spooky!" Maddy said. She still felt a bit trembly after the crevasse.

A moment later Sesame's sharp eyes spotted a paw mark in the snow, then another and another. They were huge – about the size of dinner plates! She nudged Maddy, and together they picked out a trail of paw prints, winding through the trees.

"Let's follow them," said Sesame. "You never know, they might lead us to the charm or the grotto—"

"Or a grizzly beast with fangs!" said Maddy.

"True," she said. "But it's a risk we've got to take. I've got a feeling we'll be lucky. Remember the Ice Maiden told us to keep our ears and eyes open for clues? Well, I reckon this is one of them."

Maddy knew it was useless to argue. Once Sesame had made up her mind to do something, there was no holding her back!

Six

The cave was covered in a mantle of ice and icicles hung from its mouth, like long, pointed teeth. For some time the Charmseekers followed the trail of paw prints, which eventually led them to a large cave. Now they saw a fresh track of prints leading away from the cave, and Sesame was sure that whatever had made them had recently gone out.

"*Please* be careful, Ses!" said Maddy, as she watched her disappear inside.

"It's empty," said Sesame. "Oh, Maddy. Come and see!"

As she entered the cave, Maddy ducked to avoid a needle-sharp icicle and found Sesame standing next to some fantastic ice formations, rising from the rocky floor, like strange sculptures.

"Funky!" she exclaimed.

Beneath her jacket, Sesame felt her necklace warm against her neck – it was unusually warm and tingling! Her tummy flipped. Was it another clue?

Maybe the snowflake charm was here! No, there was something else. A voice. She could hear an eerie voice inside her head and it sounded familiar.

"Pillars of ice! Pillars of ice!"

"What's up, Ses?" asked Maddy, breaking into her thoughts. "You've got one of your funny looks."

"Weird," said Sesame, shaking her head. "I thought I was on to something. I was convinced we'd find the snowflake charm here, but maybe . . ."

Her words trailed off, leaving Maddy bemused.

"What *are* you babbling about?" she said.

"Sorry," said Sesame. "I heard someone saying 'pillars of ice' and I thought—"

"*That's* what the gatekeeper said we'd turn into if we touched the wrong crystals!" said Maddy.

"Of course!" said Sesame. "It must have been a warning."

The girls tried to imagine what it would be like to be frozen forever as columns of solid ice, and shuddered at the thought. Was this what fate had in store for them?

"Come on," said Sesame, hastily brushing the horrid thoughts aside. "There's no point hanging around here.

35

We must look for the charm and those three crystals!"

"*And* be back by the Meeting of the Moons," added Maddy. "How will we know when that is?"

Instinctively Sesame glanced at her cool new watch, and was not surprised to see that the dial had changed. The digital display had been replaced with an image of two moons, drifting across a starry sky. They appeared to be gradually moving closer together, just as the Ice Maiden had described.

"I reckon they're about halfway to the eclipse," she said.

"Right," said Maddy. "Let's get going!"

The girls hurried along a labyrinth of rocky passages, taking them deeper and deeper inside the mountain. Eventually they came to a flight of stone steps. At the bottom, Sesame and Maddy found themselves standing in an enormous grotto with a frozen lake in the middle. It was like a cathedral of shimmering green ice and the beauty of it took their breath away.

"Amazing!" said Sesame.

"Fabulous!" said Maddy.

Awestruck, they gazed upwards. A large number of stalactites hung from the roof, and below each one dangled a sparkling crystal.

"Oh!" sighed Maddy. "It's like a beautiful chandelier."

Sesame nodded. She loved the way the crystals seemed to dance, their rainbow colours gleaming with every twist and twirl.

"Let's take a closer look," she said. "We may find the magic crystals the Ice Maiden needs here."

They slid across the lake until they were standing just below the chandelier. Curiously Sesame and Maddy found they could reach the crystals easily – although they didn't dare touch them. They didn't need reminding of their fate, if they should choose the wrong ones!

"How are we supposed to know which are the crystals we need?" said Maddy. "The Ice Maiden didn't say. They all look the same to me."

But Sesame had been examining them more closely.

"No, they're different," she said. "There's a star, a round one, a triangle, a diamond and—"

"You're right!" said Maddy. "They *are* different. But how does that help us pick the right crystals?"

"Hm," said Sesame. "Let me think. They're special, right?"

Maddy nodded and Sesame continued with her theory:

"I reckon they'll be different to all the others. They'll have a *special* shape of their own!"

"Cool," said Maddy. "So, if you're right, we're looking for three crystals with the *same* shape but not like any of the others?"

"Got it in one!" said Sesame.

They searched and searched among the sparkling crystals, until Sesame gave an excited squeal.

"Here's a different one, Maddy," she said. "Look, it's got six sides and it's much brighter than the others. It *must* be a magic crystal!"

"Ooo," said Maddy. "You could be right."

"Only one way to find out—" said Sesame.

"Wait!" said Maddy, panicking. The gatekeeper's dire warning was ringing in her ears, and she was afraid Sesame would turn into a block of ice.

Maddy had never felt so helpless. She gave Sesame their Charmseekers hand sign, for luck.

"Thanks," said Sesame, returning the sign. She felt nervous too, but she wanted to reassure Maddy by trying to look and sound confident. "Here goes!"

She reached up to touch the crystal . . .

"Yesss!" cried Sesame triumphantly, when for an instant, she held the freezing crystal. It glowed with a blue light but it was SO cold, it burned her fingers.

"Here," said Maddy, quickly opening the small glass casket, so that Sesame could drop it inside. "You were brill!"

Now the girls knew what the magic crystals looked like, it didn't take long to spot the other two. Maddy found the second one, and Sesame the third. But as she placed it in the casket . . .

CRACK! CRACK! CRACK!

The frozen lake splintered beneath their feet.

Can you crack the code and arrange the symbols to make a word? Each symbol represents a letter. If you solve the puzzle correctly, you'll help the Charmseekers find the snowflake charm!

Clue:
It looks like a pillar of ice!

A – heart	**N** – mermaid
B – horseshoe	**O** – butterfly
C – star	**P** – gate
D – crown	**Q** – sun
E – dolphin	**R** – moon
F – pumpkin	**S** – troll
G – fairy	**T** – cat
H – key	**U** – witch
I – candle	**V** – tree
J – coin	**W** – snowflake
K – unicorn	**X** – dragon
L – shell	**Y** – lantern
M – clover	**Z** – flower (poppy)

Seven

The girls sprang from one slab of ice to another. As they jumped on each one, symbols appeared in the ice.

"I think it's a code," said Maddy, springing to the next slab.

"Yes," said Sesame, landing beside her. "It looks like the one on my jewellery box!"

"I counted ten," said Maddy, as she sprang from the last slab onto firm ground.

"But they're melting! Quick, Ses. Tell me what they are. I'll draw them."

Maddy hunted around and found a sharp stone, then she drew the symbols as Sesame called them out.

Together they cracked the code.

"STALAGMITE," said Sesame. "I'm sure it's a clue to finding the charm."

"R-i-g-h-t," said Maddy. "Um, what exactly *is* a stalag-thingamy?"

"You find them in caves," said Sesame vaguely. "But I can never remember if they go up or down!"

They retraced their steps along the rocky
passageways, looking high and low for the charm.
Sesame was convinced they would find the
snowflake charm but, to her dismay, they reached
the mouth of the cave without finding anything.
Disappointed, the girls stopped to catch their
breath and Sesame checked her watch. The two
moons were moving ever closer together!

"We're running out of time," she told
Maddy. "If we don't find the charm
soon, we'll have to—"

She broke off, as icy goose pimples
prickled her spine and her necklace
tingled as before.

"Oh, Maddy," she said, clapping her hand to her forehead. "I've been so stupid! That voice in my head saying 'pillars of ice'! It wasn't a warning. It was a *clue*. And a stalagmite is just like a—"

"—Pillar of ice!" said Maddy, who had twigged the link between the clues straightaway.

They turned and looked again at the strange ice formations. Only then did Sesame see what she had missed the first time – the precious little silver snowflake charm, frozen inside the biggest stalagmite of all.

She felt a mixture of elation and frustration.

"How are we going to get it out?" she said. "The ice is so thick."

Maddy gave the pillar a kick.

"Ouch!"

"Ssh!" said Sesame. "What was that?"

"My foot—" began Maddy. And stopped.

Together they felt the floor vibrate, then the bulk of something unimaginably big entered the cave. Sesame stifled a scream and grabbed hold of Maddy. A gigantic bear was standing on its hind legs, towering over them.

Hot breath steamed from its muzzle and gaping jaws revealed rows of sharp, white teeth. The Charmseekers had come face to face with Karvig the Snow Bear!

"What are you doing in MY cave!" growled Karvig.

"P-p-please," said Sesame. "We came to find the snowflake charm."

"And help the Ice Maiden," added Maddy, in a small, frightened voice.

At the mention of the gatekeeper's name, the Snow Bear's attitude changed dramatically.

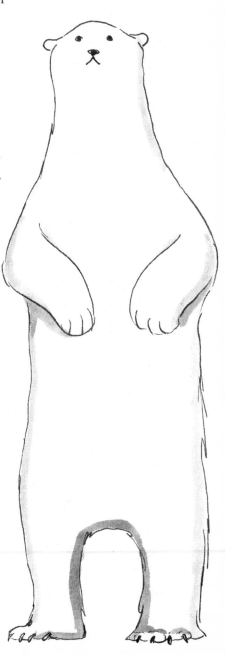

"A-a-a-a-h, the Ice Maiden!" he said sadly, his warm breath filling the cave. "She is a good friend. But she is in a bad way. Soon she will be no more . . ."

"You must be Karvig!" said Sesame, remembering the gatekeeper had mentioned him. The girls introduced themselves and Maddy held up the glass casket for the bear to see.

"These crystals will stop the Ice Maiden melting," she said. "We must hurry or—"

"I shall take you to her at once!" said Karvig.

But Sesame held up her hand.

"I'm not leaving without the charm!" she said firmly, and showed Karvig where it was trapped. The Snow Bear looked at the glittering snowflake encased in its prison of ice and shook his head in disbelief.

"A charm in my cave? Right under my nose!" he said. "I think I can help you set it free."

He took deep breaths and breathed out hot, steamy air again and again. Gradually the pillar of ice began to melt and it went on melting, until Sesame could reach the precious charm and release it.

"At last!" she said, holding the perfect little silver snowflake in the palm of her hand. For a few minutes they all admired its filigree pattern and saw how it shimmered with a magical light of its own, then Sesame put it safely in her pocket.

"*Now* we can go!" she said.

Eight

Zorgan had not been prepared for the Silversmith's ability to read his mind.

"Hm!" he murmured. "I should not have underestimated her mystic powers. In a careless moment I allowed her to gain an insight into my thoughts. Blatz!* Now she knows some of my plans. I *must* get Sesame's locket somehow."

When the magician peered into his crystal ball, he couldn't believe his luck. There was Sesame and her friend. They were in the Ice Country, riding on a Snow Bear.

* * * * * * *
✶ Blatz – a really angry exclamation

"Ah-ha!" he cried. "My chance has come, sooner than I thought . . ."

"That was SO scary!" said Maddy, when they were safely over the crevasse. She looked back at the ice bridge shimmering in the moonlight, where on either side, depths of nothingness had been ready to swallow them up. Maddy had one arm wrapped around Sesame's waist; in the other she held the casket, containing the three crystals. Sesame half-turned and nodded.

"Yeah!" she said. "I'm glad that's over." Her cheeks were glowing from the cold night air. She looked up at the two moons, drifting across the sky. "Will we make it in time, Karvig?"

"I'll do my best," said the Snow Bear.

Karvig had insisted on taking the Charmseekers to the gate. He knew the way like the back of his paws, and as they went along he talked:

"I want to help the Ice Maiden. And the sooner all the magical charms are together again, the better. Our lives depend upon it! Until that day, my beloved Ice Country remains in danger of being destroyed. Grrr! If only I could get my teeth into the cursed magician who started all this—"

"Do you mean Zorgan?" Sesame asked.

She buried her hands in Karvig's long fur. It was warm and had a musky smell.

Karvig snorted in disgust.

"That's the one," he said. "Ha! I know a story about *him*!"

"Go on," said Maddy. "We'd love to hear it."

"It happened one moonlit night," he began. "It was autumn, in the mede of Arez. The first snow had fallen and the two moons were casting their silvery-blue light over everything. It was a perfect night for hunting! I set off through the forest, hoping to pick up the scent of my supper. After a while I saw my friend Talisk, the clawbeak,* hovering in the sky— "

"Excuse me," said Sesame. "What is a clawbeak?"

"A bird with snowy white wings," said Karvig. "Talisk's eyes are so sharp she can spot a whisker twitch. She doesn't miss a thing! I couldn't find anything in the forest that night, so I walked until I reached the edge of the Ice Country. And that's when I saw it."

* *

*Clawbeak – a type of eagle. This majestic bird lives in the Snowflake Mountains of the Ice Country

"What?" asked Maddy.

"The black tower," said Karvig. "It rose from the ground, like a cobra ready to strike. I saw Zorgan throwing what *looked* like stars from the top. I knew it was Zorgan, because my mother had told me stories about him when I was a cub. I remember there was one about the Sky Dancers. That's what we call the flashing lights in the sky. You may have seen them?"

"Yes," said Sesame. "They're amazing."

"Well," Karvig continued. "My mother said that whenever I saw them, I should think of Zorgan in his dark tower casting spells. She said he was trying to challenge the beauty of the Sky Dancers and gain more power for himself. So that night, when I saw him flinging stars about, I said to myself, 'Ah,

Zorgan is making magic. I must take care!' I only discovered my mistake later. Those weren't stars. They were charms!"

"Oh!" exclaimed Sesame. "So *that's* how they were lost. But why did he throw them away?"

Karvig grunted.

"Good question," he said. "Only Zorgan knows the answer to that!"

"How did you find out they *were* charms?" asked Maddy.

"I met Talisk on my way home," said Karvig. "By then we'd both had a good night's hunting and there was time to talk. She told me she'd counted thirteen silver charms, flying like shooting stars all over Karisma."

Maddy groaned.

"No wonder they're so hard to find!" she said.

Sesame felt the snowflake charm lying safely in her pocket.

"But we *will* find them," she said confidently.

The beasts took them all completely by surprise. They came out of nowhere, their eyes red as hot coals and their piercing screeches cutting the air, like a knife.

"Shriekers!" * growled Karvig. "I might have known. Hold tight!"

There were three of them, all females – the ruthless hunters of the pack. For a while they had been waiting, crouching low, watching the Snow Bear steadily lolloping across the snowfields towards them. Food was scarce and they were hungry! The bear was huge, but they judged they could take him on. And when the time was right – they SPRANG!

* *
* Shriekers – ferocious wild dogs like wolves, so called because of the high-pitched shriek they make in full cry

Sesame and Maddy screamed as the leader leaped at Karvig's throat. They clung on as the Snow Bear reared, slashing with his blue-black claws and sending the shrieker flying. The other two circled Karvig, trying to confuse him. Suddenly one of them darted in and snapped at his leg, so Sesame kicked out as hard as she could. She caught the shrieker *smack* on the nose and saw it fall back, yelping. Meanwhile Maddy was doing her best to scare the third one off by shouting.

"Go away! *Shooo! SHOOO!*

SHOOO!"

Karvig's fury at being attacked only added to his strength. He snarled and took on all three shriekers at once, swiping, biffing and punching them with his paws, like the prizefighter he was. It didn't take them long to realise they were no match for the bear, and with shrieks and yelps they ran off to their den to lick their wounds.

"Hooray!" cried Sesame and Maddy.

"I don't think they'll be bothering us again," said Karvig. "Now, let's get on. We're nearly there!"

Sesame glanced at her watch. She reckoned they had about five minutes before the Meeting of the Moons!

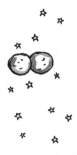

Nine

In her workshop at the foot of Mount Fortuna, the Silversmith lit a tinder-stick of mystica.* Soon the air filled with a fragrant aroma, which calmed her. Since her mind-battle with Zorgan, her thoughts have been racing. She has been gripped by a sense of foreboding, because she knows her Seeker is in great danger. Her fear of what might happen if Zorgan were to succeed trickles down her spine like melted ice.

"I *must* help her," said the Silversmith, placing her fingertips to her temples. She closed her eyes and concentrated her energies on Sesame and her

* **Mystica** – an aromatic plant, native to Karisma. The petals produce a sweet smell when burned

silver locket, then murmured, half in a trance: "If only I can reach her. Are my powers strong enough? I must put them to the test . . ."

Meanwhile Zorgan was observing the Charmseekers' progress through his powerful telescope. He had been biding his time, waiting for the right moment to strike. So when, by chance, the shriekers attacked the Snow Bear, the magician was delighted.

"Spallah!" * he exclaimed, stepping back from the spyglass to plot his next move. The pixie, Dina, stood alert, waiting for his command.

"Those mangy beasts will soon bring the bear down," muttered Zorgan, rubbing his hands with glee. "Then the Charmseekers will have to *walk* to the gate." He turned to fix Dina with a terrifying glare. "So, you'll have plenty of time to snatch Sesame's locket!"

"Yes, Master!" said Dina, her eyes glinting with eager anticipation. She couldn't wait to carry out her mission. "Leave Sesame Brown to me—"

* *
* Spallah – excellent! A triumphant expression

"Wait!" cried Zorgan. He put one eye to the telescope again and was just in time to see the shriekers beating a hasty retreat. "Blatz!" he cursed. "The Snow Bear is stronger than I thought. I must do something to stop Sesame reaching the gate. Dina, go NOW! Bring me the locket. Woe betide you if you fail!"

As soon as Dina had gone, Zorgan opened his *Book of Foul Weather Spells* and hastily thumbed through the pages. When he'd found a spell to suit his purpose, he took a deep breath and began to intone:

"Come icy blast and stinging snow . . ."

The Ice Maiden waited anxiously for the Charmseekers to return. She knew the terrible risk they had been willing to take to save her. As she waited, she wondered if they had found the crystals. And if they had, would they get back in time? Her strength was failing fast. The constant *drip, drip, drip* of her melt-water tears had weakened her, and with every drop that ran down her cheeks, she became weaker still. So, when she saw the girls riding on Karvig's back and fast approaching the gate, her hopes were raised – hopes that suddenly vanished before her eyes . . .

Only a grickle * ago she'd heard Sesame call out to her, and had seen Maddy holding up the casket with the crystals inside! Such a short distance separated them she could almost *feel* the coldness of the crystals through the glass. But out of the blue – out of a clear, cloudless night sky – came a howling wind

* *
Grickle — about the same time as a second in our world

59

that whipped the snow into a violent storm. When she looked again, Sesame, Maddy and the Snow Bear had disappeared in a blur of white.

❄

Zorgan's blizzard struck with such force, it stopped the Snow Bear in his tracks. Karvig could barely see his paw in front of his nose.

"I've known bad weather in my time," he growled. "But nothing like this!"

"Ow! That hurt," shrieked Maddy, as a blast of hailstones struck her full in the face.

"I can't see a thing," cried Sesame, above the whistling of the wind.

Then, out of the whiteness came Dina, her steely wings buzzing like an angry bee. Dina's sharp eyes spotted Sesame's locket, and she zoomed in to snatch it. Before Sesame realised what was happening, she felt a sharp tug at her neck.

"What the——?" she began.

"OWWWOOOO!"

howled Dina, recoiling. "That was HOT!"

Sesame peered through the whirling snowflakes, trying to catch a glimpse of her attacker. Then she saw a pixie with flaming red hair, blowing hard on her fingers.

"Dina!" she exclaimed. Her first thought was to protect the snowflake charm and she held it tight in her pocket. She'd had the misfortune to meet Dina twice before, when the pixie had tried to take the horseshoe and cat charms from her, so she knew how determined Dina could be. But when the pixie dived again at her throat, Sesame realised she was more interested in her necklace. Zorgan's other pixie, Nix, had tried to grab it the last time she was in Karisma. How odd, she thought, now doing her best to defend herself. Dina made to grab the locket and again she jinxed back, squealing.

The pixie was baffled. Sesame's locket was shimmering with heat. It was scorching hot! But I *must* get it, she told herself. She could hear Zorgan's threat ringing in her ears. 'Woe betide you if you fail!' She flew at Sesame once more, screaming at the top of her voice:

"Give me your locket! My master Zorgan MUST have it."

But Sesame was ready for her this time. She held on to her locket with the pictures of her parents inside, and would not let go. It felt smooth to her touch and tingled, as if her mum and dad were close by. She could almost *feel* them giving her courage.

"Well, tell Zorgan he can't have it!" she cried.

And she gave Dina a push.

Ten

While Sesame had been wrestling with Dina, Maddy and the Snow Bear had succeeded in making their way to the gate. The sudden and extraordinary turn of events happened like this:

At the very moment Dina had first swooped to snatch Sesame's locket, Maddy noticed a change in the crystals. They had started to glow, and they grew brighter and brighter, until they dazzled her with their ice-blue brilliance.

"Fantastic!" she said. "They'll show us the way to the gate."

She slid off Karvig's back, clutching the casket. "Come on," she said to the Snow Bear. "We must hurry!"

The crystals shone a path of light through the raging blizzard and when they reached the gate, everything happened at once. Sesame pushed Dina away and jumped to the ground. She just had time to give Karvig a hug and whisper something in his ear, before running with Maddy to the gate.

"Thank you!" said the Ice Maiden, as Maddy handed her the casket. As soon as she opened the lid, the crystals burst into a shower of tiny freezing stars and swathed her in an icy mist. It was SO cold, it took the girls' breath away, but it stopped the beautiful maiden from melting. She beamed at the Charmseekers, as she held the gate open for them. "Did you find the snowflake charm?" she asked.

Sesame patted her pocket.

"Yes!" she said, her eyes sparkling with delight.

"I thought you would," said the Ice Maiden, with a knowing smile. "Now, hurry. It's time to go. Setfair,✶ Charmseekers. Come back soon!"

* *

✶ Setfair – goodbye and good luck

65

As Sesame and Maddy fell into a fluffy cloud of soft white snow they saw the two moons of Karisma slip one behind the other. The very last thing they heard was a roar from the Snow Bear, as Karvig sent Dina spinning, in a blast of hot air!

The girls fell into the snowdrift with a *CRUMP!* Sesame and Maddy looked up, to find Nic looking down at them. He'd just taken their photograph.

"Great!" he said. "This one's definitely for the front page."

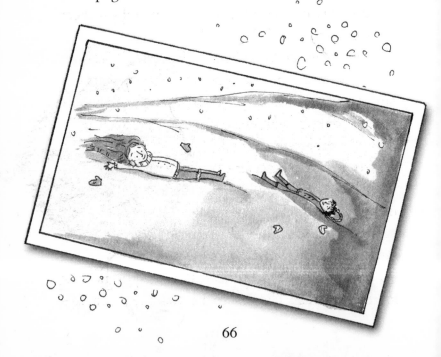

Sesame struggled to her feet in a daze.

"No way, Dad!" she said. "I'd be SO embarrassed!"

"Me too," said Maddy, her head in a spin.

"Thought I'd lost you for a minute," he said, turning the camera round, to show them the picture. "Deep snowdrift! Anyway, time to go. I think you've had enough snow for one day."

Sesame and Maddy looked at each other. If only he knew what an amazing adventure they'd just had.

Later, after they'd taken Maddy home and Sesame was alone in her room, she took the precious silver snowflake from her pocket and looked at its delicate pattern again. Flashbacks of what they'd been through raced inside her head.

"But it was worth it!" she told Alfie, as she opened her jewellery box. Carefully she placed the glistening snowflake with the other six charms and the silver bracelet she'd already found and firmly closed the lid. "I know much more about these charms now," she said. "I can't wait to go back and look for the others! It's really important for the thirteen charms to be together, you see?

Terrible things are happening in Karisma because they've been lost. All because of that horrid magician Zorgan. I can't *believe* he threw them away!"

As soon as she said his name, images of her struggle with Dina flashed before her eyes. This was the second time one of Zorgan's pixies had tried to snatch her necklace, and she couldn't think why the magician would want it. It was weird the way it had burned the pixie too. She undid the clasp and laid her necklace beside her jewellery box. As she did so, the locket suddenly sprang open and there were the tiny pictures of her parents, smiling back at her.

Sesame looked at them fondly. She loved her dad *so* much, but she missed not having her mum around. She thought Poppy looked beautiful. Gently she closed the locket. It was one of her most treasured possessions.

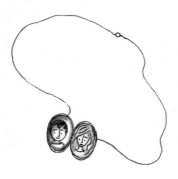

Eleven

The Silversmith goes to her window in time to see the two moons, passing one behind the other. "Quisto!"* she exclaims. "The Meeting of the Moons. Who knows what strange things have happened beneath your beams this night?"

She turns from the window, and as she looks at the thirteen magic candles, she gives a sigh of relief.

"One thing I know for sure," she says. "The snowflake charm has been found!" For she sees the flame of the candle that bears its name has died. Now six candles remain burning brightly, six glowing beacons of hope that will burn until their charms have been found.

The Silversmith reflects on her exhausting encounters with Zorgan earlier in the day.

* * * * * * * * * * * * * * * * * *

Quisto – an exclamation of surprise

"I thwarted his attempts to discover where Sesame is keeping the charms," she says to herself. "Perish the day he ever finds out about the jewellery box! He will stop at nothing to possess the charms. Worse still, if he *should* get hold of Sesame's locket—"

A shiver runs down her spine. The consequences are too awful to think about. But she draws comfort from knowing she's protected her Seeker – this time. She allows herself a smile of satisfaction, as she imagines how surprised Dina must have been to burn her fingers on the locket.

Perhaps Zorgan's little pixie won't be quite so eager next time, she thinks. Although she fears deep down there *will* be a next time, and that Sesame remains in great danger, as she continues her quest.

But that is another story! It must be told another day.